The Little Book of

Zombie

Mathematics

25 Zombie-based maths problems

ISBN - 978-1-909832-21-3
Published by Pictish Beast Publications, Glasgow, UK.
Printed in the United Kingdom
First Printing: 2015. First Edition.

www.ForThoseInPeril.net/mathswithzombies.htm

Cover Image: Original artwork created specifically for this book © 2013, Colin M. Drysdale

By the same Author:

For Grown-ups:
(or those who feel they're grown-up)

The *For Those in Peril* series:

For Those in Peril on the Sea
The Outbreak
The Island at the End of the World

Other Books:

Zombies can't swim and Other Tales of the Undead

For Children:
(or those who, deep inside, feel that they're still children)

Zombies Love Brains (coming soon)

These books are available from *Pictish Beast Publications* in paperback and/or as Kindle ebooks.

Contents

Part Two: The Answers

Part Three: Your MWZ Score

Preface

I've had an unhealthy addiction to recreational mathematics for many years. I even own a book titled *Curious and Interesting Geometry,* and I'm proud enough about it to admit this in public. However, I can see why many people have a very different relationship with mathematics from me. This, I strongly believe, has nothing to do with any innate mathematical ability, but rather is to do with the way that maths is taught in most Western countries. Teachers are so consumed by the need to teach particular skills and hit specific milestones that they manage to drain all the fun out of maths.

If there was a precise moment in my life at which the idea for this volume was conceived it was after reading a book by Robert Smith? — yes, the question mark is meant to be there — called *Braaaiiinnnsss!: From Academics to Zombies.* At that point, I'd just completed my first zombie-based, post-apocalyptic survival novel (*For Those in Peril on the Sea*), mostly as an antidote to my time working in academia, and I realised that using zombie scenarios would be a great way of getting people, who might otherwise never consider it, interested in maths. Thus, I started writing maths-based zombie scenarios. The more I wrote, the more I realised I could combine two of the main passions in my life — maths and zombies — and hopefully, use people's interest in the latter to make them interested in the former. I knew it might be a long shot, but what did I have to lose? The result was the *Maths with Zombies* blog on which this book is based.

This book wouldn't have been possible without contributions from a wide range of people (some of whom know about this, and others won't). Firstly, I need to thank Johnny Ball. As a kid I was obsessed with him, and I don't think I'd ever have developed such an interest in mathematics without his influence. There was also the primary school teacher who first introduced me to the *Four Colour Theorem* (see Problem 25), whose name sadly I can't remember, and I can only apologise for that. The variation on the *Königsberg Bridge Problem* which I present in Problem 24, was inspired by an episode of Dara O'Briain's *School of Hard Sums*. The rest pretty much comes from my rather fertile imagination.

In terms of people that I actually *know*, thanks to Stephen Burges for checking all the maths and correcting me when I'd got things wrong (and for not gloating too much about this on the few occasions when this happened!), to Gale Winskill of Winskill Editorial (*www.winskilleditorial.co.uk*) for editing this volume (any editing issues which remain in this volume are when I have unwisely over-ruled her sage advice), and most of all to Sarah, for putting up with my twin obsessions with zombies (which she shares) and recreational mathematics (which she doesn't).

Introduction

Maths is boring, right? Well … yes, especially when it's all about how long it takes train A to pass train B given their relative speeds. So, so boring and not exactly relevant to real life, is it? The thing is, it needn't be this way. Maths problems can be made both much more interesting and more relevant to everyday life. How? By adding zombies! Zombies make everything better and, of course, as we all know, one day there will be a zombie apocalypse. When that happens the maths problems in this book are the ones you'll need to be able to solve if you want to survive in a world where the dead walk again ...

This is the world of *Maths with Zombies*. Enjoy!

***

The book is split into three parts. Part One contains the problems. For each problem, you'll be presented with a scenario that you might encounter in a zombie apocalypse, which you can solve using mathematics. If you don't fancy doing the maths, don't worry, multiple choice answers are provided for each one and you can just guess ... but I wouldn't recommend doing that if you encounter such situations for real during a zombie apocalypse!

In Part Two, you'll find the answers. Here, you are given both the correct answer and information on how you could've worked it out using mathematics. If you're not interested in knowing this, there's no need for you to read this information, but why not read it anyway? You never know, you might find some useful zombie-apocalypse survival tips in amongst the maths.

There are two ways you can work through this book. Firstly, you can just treat each scenario as an independent maths problem or, indeed, a zombie-apocalypse survival problem. Secondly, and perhaps more interestingly, you can treat all the problems as a single test of how well your maths ability will help you survive in the almost inevitable event of a zombie apocalypse. The right answer for each problem has a *Maths with Zombies* (MWZ) points value associated with it, based on how hard, or how easy, it is to work it out. Keep a note of the points your score for each problem and once you've finished all 25, add them up to get your overall MWZ score.

Once you've got this, go to Part Three (which starts on page 85), where you will find information about what your MWZ score means for your chances of survival in the event of the dead suddenly coming back to life.

***

These maths problems originate from the *Maths with Zombies* blog written by Colin M. Drysdale (*MathsWithZombies.wordpress.com*), and all the problems in this book are already freely available on that site. This book simply brings them all together in one place and makes them easier to work through when you have a few spare moments, and fancy dipping into the weird and wonderful world of zombie mathematics.

Part One

The Problems

1. The Reload Problem

There are 50 zombies staggering towards you. You have a gun that holds 6 bullets and it's fully loaded (after all, there are zombies out there so you'd make very sure you were fully prepared before stepping out of your safe house). Assuming you don't miss with any of your shots — and you'd better not or the zombies will get you! — how many times will you have to reload your gun before you've killed them all?

A. 6
B. 7
C. 8
D. 9

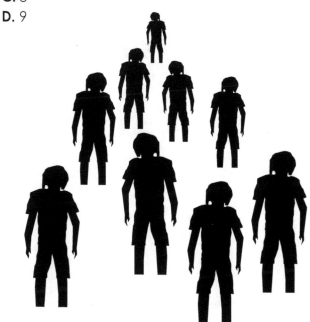

2. The Hit And Miss Problem

There are 20 walking dead coming up the street towards your house. You know you need to shoot the zombies in the head to kill them, but you're scared — who wouldn't be in this situation? — so your aim is off. This means there's only a 60% chance of you killing a zombie with each shot. What's the fewest number of shots you'll need to fire before you are certain to have killed them all?

A. 32
B. 34
C. 33
D. 35

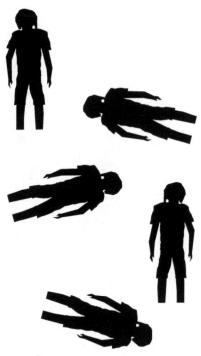

3. The Fuel Crisis Problem

You hear the first reports on the news that the dead have started to rise and attack the living. You knew this was going to happen and you're ready. You grab your 'bug-out bag' and a baseball bat before leaping into your car. The safe house you've been carefully preparing and provisioning for the last year is 74 miles away and if you drive fast enough you'll be there in an hour at the most; then you'll be safe. As you start your engine you glance at the fuel gauge. That's when you realise your room mate's not only borrowed your car yet again without asking, but he's also not topped up the tank so it's only a quarter full. You know your tank holds 11 gallons when it's full and your car does 27 miles to the gallon. What do you do?

A. I've got enough fuel to get to my safe house, so I'm leaving the city while I still can.

B. There's not enough fuel left in the tank. I'll need to get some more before I head off. It'll be risky but at least I won't end up stranded in the middle of nowhere when I run out.

9

4. The Viral Spread Problem

There's a virus turning people into zombies that attack the living and never die. No one knows where it came from, but the first person — known as 'patient zero' by those who study how diseases spread — was an archaeologist who'd just discovered an ancient tomb, so it might have come from there. The virus is spread when infected people bite someone who's uninfected. If each zombie bites an average of 3 uninfected people each day, how long will it take before the entire human population of the planet — which, for this problem, will be taken as 7 billion people — is turned into shambling undead flesh-munchers?

> **A.** 167 days (almost 6 months)
> **B.** 53 days (just under 8 weeks)
> **C.** 17 days (just over two weeks)
> **D.** 6 days (less than a week)

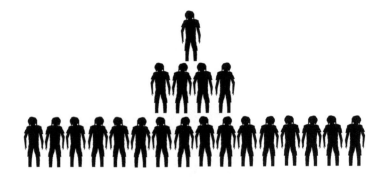

5. The Hungry Zombies Problem

There are 5 million people in your city and 25 graveyards. Each graveyard has an average of 5,000 graves in it, and when the zombie apocalypse comes, the dead in all these graves will rise up and attack the living. How many people will each zombie have to consume before there's no one left alive in the city?

    A. 10
    B. 40
    C. 100
    D. 400

6. The Injured Friend Problem

You can see the zombies staggering towards you. You estimate that they're moving at 4 miles an hour. Normally, you'd be able to outrun them no problem, but today you're carrying your best friend, who's just broken his leg and can't walk. This means you can only move at 1 mile an hour. He might be your friend, but he's heavy! You can see the door to your safe house at the end of the street. It's 83 yards away. You look back over your shoulder: the zombies are 200 yards behind you. You have two options: you can carry on with your friend, but he'll slow you down; or you can abandon him to his certain death so you can move faster. If you keep carrying your friend, will you still make it to your safe house before the zombies get to you? **Hint:** There are 1,760 yards in a mile.

- **A.** Yes, so the best thing to do is keep carrying my friend. After all, I can't just abandon him to his certain, and gruesome, death.
- **B.** No, so the only way I'll survive is if I abandon my friend so I can run faster. I'll miss him, but it's better than ending up being torn to pieces by a horde of marauding zombies.

7. The Rapid Fire Problem

You are armed with a machine gun that can fire 131 bullets per minute. That's a lot of bullets, but it's not very accurate and you only hit 30% of the zombies you fire it at. Suddenly, a swarm of 400 zombies appears over a nearby hill and they're moving quickly (they're those pesky new fast zombies!). You estimate they'll be at the gates of your compound in 10 minutes, and if that happens, you'll be overrun. Is there enough time to kill all the zombies with your machine gun before they get there? If there is, your best option is to stand and fight. If not, you should run now. You'll have to leave all your supplies and gear behind, and start afresh somewhere new. It won't be easy, but at least you'll be alive!

A. I'll get them all just in time, so my best option is to stay and fight.

B. There's not enough time to kill all the zombies before they get here, so I need to get out now.

8. The Quick Draw Problem

You're on your own in a dark alley when a zombie suddenly spots you. It turns in your direction and charges towards you. It's 20 feet away, and since it's one of those new-fangled fast zombies again, it's moving at a speed of 9 miles an hour. You know it will take you 1.5 seconds flat to draw your gun, aim and fire. Will you have time to kill the zombie before it gets to you? **Hint:** There are 5,280 feet in a mile.

A. There isn't enough time to shoot the zombie, I'd better start running. Fast.

B. I've got enough time so I should stand my ground and kill the zombie.

9. The Food Supply Problem

The zombie apocalypse has come, and you find yourself all alone and barricaded into an old house. You don't know who lived there before, but they kept their cupboards well-stocked. You count everything that's in them and find you've got 56 cans of food. Unfortunately, they're all Spam, but it's better than nothing[1]. You read the label and find that each can weighs 200g and contains 621 calories. You know you need to eat 2,500 calories each day to stay healthy. How many days can you survive on your supply of Spam before you have to go outside, where the zombies are, in search of food?

A. 13 days
B. 15 days
C. 17 days
D. 19 days

---

[1] Not that there is anything wrong with Spam. I'm sure it's a perfectly nice product. it's just not my cup of tea!

10. The Disappearing Zombies Problem

The apocalypse has come and, with the exception of a few small, scattered groups of survivors, the entire population of the world has been turned into zombies. That means there are 7 billion undead walking around, looking for human flesh on which to feast. You're lucky enough to be holed up in an old military bunker you stumbled upon while escaping from the city. You know that zombies, being re-animated dead bodies, will eventually rot away, making it safe for you to go outside again. You work out that zombies have a half-life of 28 days. This means that every 28 days the number of zombies remaining will decrease by 50%. How long will be before all the zombies are gone and it's safe for you to go outside again?

A. 364 days
B. 756 days
C. 924 days
D. 1,120 days

11. The Fork In The Road Problem

You've been caught out in the open while foraging for food. You're at a fork in the road, with the zombies coming from the south, and they are 100 yards away from you. You have two options, both of which lead to a safe house. On the road to the north-east, there's a safe house only 100 yards away, but it's up a steep hill. To the north-west, there's another safe house. It's further away (some 300 yards), but it's all downhill. You know you can run at 11.25 miles an hour downhill, but only 7.5 miles an hour uphill. The zombies are relentless and can move at 15 miles an hour, regardless of whether they're going uphill or downhill. Which way should you go? **Hint:** There are 1,760 yards in a mile.

A. Northwest: it's further but I can run faster down hill so I'd get there quicker.
B. Northeast: the safe house is nearer so even though running uphill is slower, I'd get there quicker.
C. It doesn't matter which way I go, I'll still make it to a safe house first, as long as I don't waste time trying to work out which way I should go.

17

D. It doesn't matter which way I go, given how fast the zombies can run, they'll get me before I reach a safe house.

E. Regardless of which road I take, it'll be a dead heat. We'll all reach the door at the same time, but that doesn't matter because I'll still end up dead: in the case of a draw, the zombies always win!

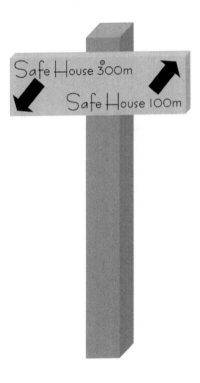

12. The Prius vs SUV Problem

The dead have risen and you want to get as far away as possible, as quickly as possible. You run out of your house to look for some transport. You can only find two possible cars: an SUV with its 42-gallon fuel tank two-thirds full, and a Prius with 9 gallons of fuel in it. The SUV does 14 mpg (miles per gallon), while the Prius does 36 mpg[2]. Which vehicle will allow you to get further away from the zombie outbreak on just the fuel in its tank?

- **A.** The SUV: it uses more fuel per mile, but with all that fuel in the tank, it'll get me further.
- **B.** The Prius: there's less fuel in it, but it does more miles to the gallon and that will mean I can get further away.

[2] I'm sure a real Prius does better mileage than this, but we're talking about a zombie apocalypse here, so I'm allowed to take a little bit of artistic licence with such things.

13. The Amputation Problem

You look at the bite on your hand and know instantly you've been infected. You know the virus spreads through your body along your lymph vessels, and that once it reaches your heart, it will empty into your blood system, and then it will be too late to do anything about it. You know the virus travels through your lymph system at 2.8 inches per second, and that your arm is 16 inches long. How long do you have to amputate your arm before this 'treatment' becomes ineffective because the virus has already reached your heart? **Note:** You will need to do the maths and amputate your arm in this time, so you'll need to work out the correct answer very quickly or you won't have time to act.

A. 5 seconds
B. 10 seconds
C. 15 seconds
D. 20 seconds

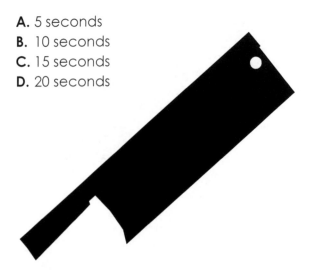

14. The Zombie Abundance Problem

You are an army general trying to work out how many soldiers you need to clear a city of zombies. To have any chance of taking the city back, past experience has told you that you need to have at least 1 soldier for every 10 zombies: anything less than that and you won't succeed. However, if you send in too many men, you'll leave your base without enough soldiers to protect it should zombies attack. This means you need to send in exactly the right number of soldiers: no more, no less. To get an estimate of the number of zombies in the city, you've sent out a helicopter to count the number of zombies in five randomly selected city blocks. Its crew counted 523 zombies in the first one, 632 in the second, 781 in the third, 421 in the fourth and 307 in the fifth one. Given that for every zombie seen on the streets you know there are 4 hidden from sight in the buildings, and that there are 142 similar-sized blocks in the city, how many soldiers do you need to send, to guarantee that you'll be able to take back the city without jeopardising the safety of your base?

- **A.** 2,738 soldiers
- **B.** 15,627 soldiers
- **C.** 37,829 soldiers
- **D.** 65,342 soldiers

15. The Outrunning Your Friends Problem

There are 37 zombies chasing you and your friends. The zombies are fast ones and they'll quickly catch whoever's moving slowest. Each time one of your friends gets caught, 3 zombies stop to feast on their brains. How many of your friends do you have to outrun before all the zombies are too busy eating other people to chase you, meaning you can finally get away?

  A. 12
  B. 13
  C. 14
  D. 15

16. The Wall Problem

There's been an outbreak of the zombie disease in Glasgow, and Scotland is rapidly being overrun. The latest surveillance mission spotted a horde of zombies heading south. They're currently 125 miles away and are moving at a speed of 3 miles per hour. Scotland is lost and the best way to protect the rest of Britain is to build a defensive barricade on the ruins of an ancient Roman wall which was last used over 1,600 years ago. 750 people can build a 1-mile section of 10 foot high wall in a day, but the wall will need to stretch the entire 73 miles from one side of Britain to the other, along the border between Scotland and England, if it's going to keep the zombies out. What's the minimum number of people you will need to recruit to ensure the wall's completed before the zombie horde gets to it?

    A. 7,884
    B. 15,768
    C. 31,536
    D. 54,750

17. The Tank vs Motorcycle Problem

You've heard about a safe zone which has been set up, and you figure that getting there is your best chance of surviving the zombie outbreak in your country. The bad news is that it's 125 miles away. You have two transport options: a motorbike, and a tank. The motorbike's much faster and you'll be able to travel at 60 miles per hour. However, it's also much more dangerous and there's a 1-in-6 chance you'll be grabbed by a zombie during each hour you're on the road. The tank's a lot slower and can only travel at 7 miles per hour, meaning you'll be on the road for longer, but it's also much safer and there's only a 1-in-50 chance of a zombie getting you during each hour you are travelling. Which transport option offers you the best chance of getting to the safe zone in one piece?

A. The tank's slower but safer, so it'll the best option.

B. While the motorbike is less safe, I'll get there quicker, so overall it's the best option.

24

18. The Zombie Horde Problem

You're out foraging for food when you turn a corner and find a mass of zombies staggering down the street towards you. Climbing onto a burnt-out car, you can see that the horde stretches back for 5 city blocks, each of which is 88 yards long, and that it is moving at 3 miles an hour. You look round for somewhere to hide, but the only shelter that's close enough is an abandoned tank. You climb inside and lock the hatch just as the first of the zombies reaches you. If you keep very quiet, they won't know you're there and they'll all walk right past. If, however, they realise you're inside, they'll surround the tank and you'll never be able to get out alive. Being a tank, there's no way for you to see outside without opening the hatch to take a look, yet night is falling fast and if you stay in the tank too long, you won't be able to get back to your safe house before it gets dark, so every minute counts. How long will it be before it's safe for you to open the hatch again? **Hint:** There're 1,760 yards in a mile.

- **A.** 4 minutes
- **B.** 5 minutes
- **C.** 6 minutes
- **D.** 7 minutes

19. The Containment Zone Problem - Part I

There's been a report of a zombie outbreak on the north side of the city, and your unit of 600 men has been sent in to set up a containment zone while others attempt to neutralise the problem. So far, the outbreak is limited to a single city block and your containment zone will consist of a 1-block buffer zone on all sides of the affected area. This means you will have to seal off a square consisting of a total of 9 city blocks, each of which is 50 yards long and 50 yards wide. To make sure your defences hold, you know you need to have at least 2 soldiers for every 3 yards of your perimeter. You have two choices: set up the containment zone now; or wait for reinforcements. If you try to set up the containment zone and you don't have enough men to guard it properly, you risk being overrun and the zombies will take over the city. However, any unnecessary delay while you wait for reinforcements will give the zombie disease time to spread, making it harder to contain. You're the one in charge and need to make a decision right now. Do you have enough men to set an effective containment zone or should you wait for reinforcements? You have five seconds …

> **A.** Yes, I have more than enough men and the best action is to set up the containment zone right away.

26

B. I don't have enough men under my command. It will give the zombie disease time to spread, but I need to wait until reinforcements arrive before I can set up an effective containment zone.

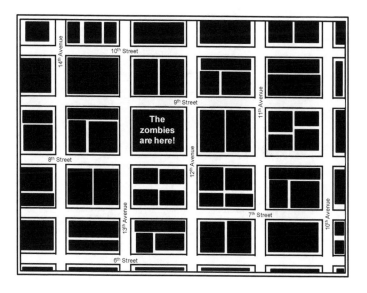

20. The Containment Zone Problem - Part II

You have a unit of 600 men under your command. You've set up a containment zone surrounding a square of 9 city blocks to contain a zombie outbreak, but somehow, one of the undead has broken through your defensive line. You give the order for your men to pull back 1 block in every direction. As before, each block is 50 yards long by 50 yards wide, and you still need at least 2 soldiers for every 3 yards of your perimeter to ensure it's secure. Do you still have enough men to guard the containment zone once you've pulled back, or should you call for reinforcements?

A: With 600 men, I can still maintain a secure containment zone even if we have to pull back.

B: Once we pull back, the perimeter will be too long for my men to guard effectively. I'll need to call for reinforcements.

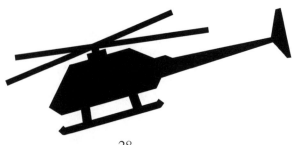

21. The Vaccination Programme Problem

Two months ago, a frightening new disease emerged from nowhere and killed several hundred people in a remote farming community before it was successfully brought under control by the army. Based on the testimony of the few survivors, this disease caused those infected with it to attack and bite anyone they could get their hands on. Those who were bitten soon started doing the same and it's no surprise that this new disease has been dubbed 'the zombie virus' by news reporters. You're worried that if a similar outbreak happened in a more heavily populated area, the disease could sweep quickly across the whole country, or maybe even the world, before it could be brought under control, and this could bring humanity to an abrupt, and rather gory, end.

After many weeks of hard work, you've created a vaccine against this new disease and you've calculated that, to be effective at stopping any further outbreaks getting out of hand and turning into a full-blown zombie apocalypse, you need to make sure that at least 95% of the population is vaccinated. It takes 6 minutes to give someone a shot and you have a team of 2,500 trained health professionals to administer the vaccine, each of whom can work for 16 hours a day. To the nearest whole day, how long will it take to vaccinate enough people in the USA (assuming a population of 250 million) to prevent a zombie apocalypse happening there?

    A. 297 days
    B. 396 days
    C. 475 days
    D. 594 days

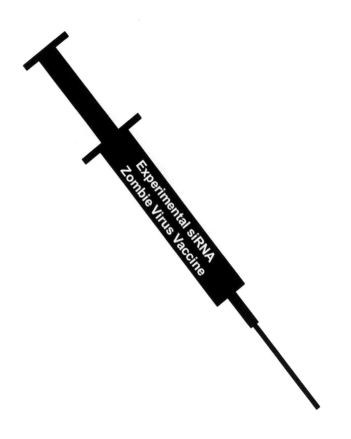

22. The Recruitment Problem

There's a zombie outbreak in a city of 15 million people. The army has been ordered to deal with it, and as the general in charge, that means you have to decide what to do. You could send in all your troops, but then you would have none to spare if there's another outbreak somewhere else. Instead, you decide to send in a skeleton force of just 1,600 soldiers, with orders to recruit members of the public to help them fight the zombies. It's a novel solution, and leaves you with plenty of men in case there are any other outbreaks, but no one else thinks it'll work. To prove them wrong, you set out to do the maths. You know that each soldier can hunt down and kill 20 zombies a day. In the evening, each soldier can also recruit 1 new soldier from the people in the city, who will join the fight the following day. However, each night the zombies will fight back and infect 5 normal people who will then become zombies. You know there are currently 50,000 zombies in the city. Have you made the right decision?

    A. Yes, the maths shows this is the right decision. It might take a while, but the strategy will work and the soldiers, with the help of their new recruits, will eventually regain control of the city.

    B. The maths shows that while the basic strategy is sound, I'd need

31

to send in more troops at the start for it to be successfully implemented.

C. No. The maths shows that this is the wrong decision. No matter how many soldiers are sent in, the strategy will never work. This is because the number of zombies keeps increasing at a rate faster than the soldiers can kill them, even with all their new recruits. The only thing which can stop the outbreak spreading is to nuke the entire city before the situation gets any worse.

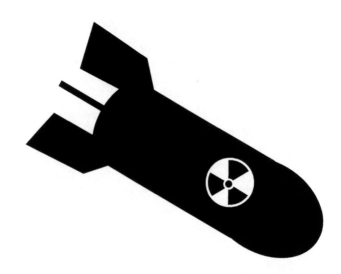

23. The Big Freeze Problem

The zombie apocalypse has begun and a large group of you has sought refuge in the far north because you've heard that zombies can't move at low temperatures, because they seize up if they get too cold. However, in the northern latitudes where you're hiding out, it's not always sufficiently cold for this to happen, and for 3 months of the year (June, July and August) the temperatures are warm enough for the zombies to advance. This is quickly becoming known as 'the walking season', and is dreaded by everyone since it's when almost all zombie attacks take place. Only 30% of the zombies survive the annual chill, and in each month, when it's warm enough for them to move, they can stagger 100 miles. It's now the end of August and the temperatures have just started to drop so the zombies have frozen up for the winter meaning this year's walking season is over. You've estimated that 2 million zombies crossed the Canadian border, heading north, just before this happened. How long will it take for this zombie horde to reach you, 1,300 miles to the north, and how many will be left when they do?

> **A.** It will take 4 years for them to reach us, and there will be 16,200 zombies left when they do.

33

B. They'll reach us in 4 years and 10 months, and there will only be 4,860 left by then.

C. It will take the zombies 5 years and 10 months to get here, and there will be 1,458 left.

D. All the zombies will die from the cold before they reach here so we're completely safe.

24. The Six Bridges Problem

You're holidaying on a small archipelago when a zombie outbreak catches you unaware. You manage to get to a safe house, but there are no supplies of any kind, and this means you'll need to go on a supply run. You look at a map of the 5 islands in the archipelago (see page 36), and see that they're connected by 6 bridges. Your safe house is on the northern-most island and you can see that there's a warehouse where you can get food and drink from on the large island to the south-west. There's also a hospital where you'll be able to get medical supplies on another large island to the south-east. Between these two large islands are a couple of small ones, one of which has a gun store on it, where you will be able to find weapons, while another has an ammunition dump, where you can get plenty of ammunition. You look out the window and see zombies shambling around. They look slow and you know you'd probably be able to outrun them, but the moment they know you're there, they'll start following you. This means that once you cross a bridge, they'll follow you onto it and you won't be able to cross it again because there will be too many zombies on it. Is there a route, starting from your safe house, which will allow you to visit all the places you need to go to for supplies, and to make it back to your safe house without having to use any of the bridges twice?

A. Yes, there's a route which allows me to visit all the places I need to go to get supplies and still get back to the safe house without having to use any of the bridges twice. I'm setting off now before things get any worse.

B. There's no route which will allow me to visit everywhere I need to go and still get back to the safe house without having to cross the same bridge twice. The most places I can visit, and still get home safely, is 3 out of the 4 locations, so I'll need to decide which one to leave out on my supply run.

Map of the Archipelago

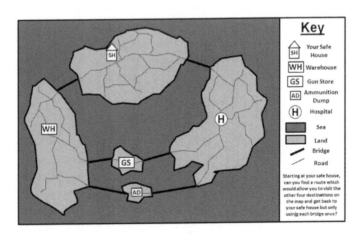

Key

Your Safe House

WH Warehouse

GS Gun Store

AD Ammunition Dump

H Hospital

Sea

Land

Bridge

Road

Starting at your safe house, can you find a route which would allow you to visit the other four destinations on the map and get back to your safe house but only using each bridge once?

25. The Colourful Hats Problem

You are the general in charge of an army division which has been assigned the task of clearing an island of zombies. To make the job easier, you've divided it into 21 zones (see the map on page 38) and assigned 1 unit of soldiers to clear each zone. The plans are all in place and the soldiers are raring to go. Before you give the order, you check everything over one last time. That's when you realise there's a problem: where one zone meets another, there's a risk of soldiers from different units getting mixed up if they run into each other, especially if it's during a battle with a zombie horde. This could leave some of the units dangerously undermanned and unable to continue with their assignment until they get their missing men back. Such confusion will slow the whole mission down, and could even result in its failure. What you need, you realise, is an easy way for the soldiers to tell which men are in which units.

Suddenly, the solution comes to you: since zombies only react to sound and movement rather than colour, there's really no need for camouflage. This means you can simply provide brightly coloured hats to each unit, and make sure that units assigned to neighbouring zones are given different coloured hats so they don't get mixed up. However, the more different colours of hats you need to order, the longer it will take to start the mission, and the more zombies there will be when the fighting starts, making it more dangerous and difficult, so speed is of the essence. Given the zones you have created, what's the minimum number of different colours of hat you'll need so that the soldiers in every zone can be assigned one that's different from those being used in all neighbouring zones?

    A. 2
    B. 3
    C. 4
    D. 5

Map of the Island showing the 21 Zones

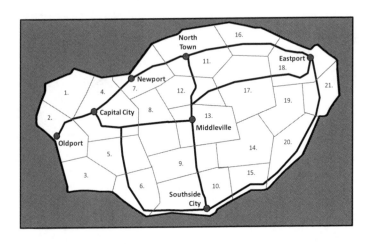

Part Two

The Answers

1. The Reload Problem

What answer did you get?

A: That's not nearly enough. There are still going to be loads of zombies coming towards you!

B: You're getting closer, but there'd still be 2 dead men walking.

C: Spot on, and you'll still have 4 bullets left in case you run into any more. **MWZ Points:** 1.

D: Whoa, calm down there! That's one too many reloads. Don't be so trigger-happy. You can't afford to waste your precious ammunition!

How to work it out: You're going to have to fire 50 shots to kill 50 zombies (we'll cover the subject of what happens if you aren't a perfect shot in Problem 2). You've got 6 bullets in your gun already, so that's 6 zombies dead before you have to reload meaning there's 44 left (50 - 6). Each time you reload the gun, you put 6 bullets into it, so if you divided 44 — the number of bullets needed to kill the rest of the undead horde — by 6 — the number of bullets the gun can hold — you get 7.333. Since you can't load a gun 0.333 times, this number needs to be rounded up to 8, and so you arrive at the answer. If there had been 48 zombies, the answer would be (48 - 6)/6, which is 7 (there's no decimal fraction so there's no need to round the answer up). If there were 52 zombies, the answer would be (52 - 6)/6, which is 7.6667, so again you'd need to reload your gun 8 times, but this time you'd only have 2 bullets left in the gun by the time they were all dead.

2. The Hit And Miss Problem

What answer did you get?

A: Oh boy, you're in trouble, there's still 1 zombie left.

B: That's perfect! All the walking dead are now ... er ... *deader?* **MWZ Points:** 1.

C: Oh so close, but there's still a small chance you'll miss the last one.

D: That's one shot too many! This is a zombie apocalypse. You can't afford to waste ammo like that!

How to work it out: A 60% chance of killing a zombie means that for every 100 shots you fire, you'll only kill 60 zombies. If you divide both these numbers by 100, you get the probability of killing a zombie with each shot (in this case, it's 0.6 for every 1 bullet fired). The minimum number of shots you'd need to fire, to make sure all the zombies are killed, is calculated by taking the number of zombies (20) and dividing it by the probability of killing a zombie each time you fire your gun (the 0.6 you worked out above). 20/0.6 is 33.3333. However, you can't fire 0.3333 of a bullet. If you round it down to 33 shots, there's a small possibility (40%) that you won't kill the last zombie (and when you're trying to survive in a zombie apocalypse you don't want that!). So you'd need to round up to 34 shots to make sure you've got the lot. Any more shots than that would just be a waste of precious ammo.

3. The Fuel Crisis Problem

What answer did you get?

A. Well done, you made the right decision. You must have correctly worked out you have enough fuel to go 74.25 miles before you run out and that's just enough to get you to your safe house. **MWZ Points:** 1.
B. Oooh, poor choice. You had enough fuel so you should've left immediately. Enjoy fighting off the zombie horde as you waste time trying to find more fuel before you leave the city.

How to work it out: You first need to work out how much fuel you have left in the tank. This is the size of the tank (11 gallons) multipled by how much is left in it (¼), which tells you that it has 2.75 gallons in it. Next you need to work out how far you can go on this much fuel. This is done by multiplying the number of miles your car can do per gallon (27) by the amount of fuel you have left (2.75 gallons). This gives you 74.25 miles. Finally, subtract the miles you have to travel from this distance (74.25 - 74). If this number is positive (as in this case here, where it's 0.25), you've got enough fuel to get you there. If it's negative, you don't. This would be the case if the miles per gallon was only 0.5 lower: (2.75 x 26.5) - 74 = -1.125, so you'd run out of fuel just over a mile from your safe house. If that were the case, you'd be better selecting option B.

4. The Viral Spread Problem

What answer did you get?

A: You're way off! You'll have no chance of stopping an outbreak if you can't work out how fast it will spread.

B: You're closer, but you're still dangerously underestimating how fast the disease will spread.

C: Spot on! Now you know exactly how long it will take before humanity is gone. **MWZ Points:** 1.

D: You're a pessimist, aren't you? The last human won't become infected for another 11 days.

How to work it out: The simplest way to work it out is to calculate the number of people infected at the end of each day, given the number of people infected at the start, and the average number of people that will be bitten, and so infected. For day 1, there will be 1 person infected at the start of the day (the unfortunate archaeologist) and he will infect 3 people by biting them. This means that at the end of the day there will be 4 zombies (1 + 3 = 4). Day 2 starts with 4 infected people, each of whom will bite and infect 3 people. That's a total of 12 people (4 x 3 = 12). Therefore, at the end of day 2 there will be a total of 16 zombies (4 + 12 = 16). If we carry this on, we'll find that at the end of day 3 there will be 64 zombies, 256 at the end of day 4, and so on, until at the start of day 17 there will be 4,294,967,296 zombies, and since there's only 7 billion people on the planet, they will run out of uninfected people to bite somewhere around lunchtime.

5. The Hungry Zombies Problem

What answer did you get?

A: That would barely make a dent in the human population of the city. There'd still be 3.75 million people left.

B: You're right, but it's not a lot that each zombie needs to eat to consume a whole city, is it?. **MWZ Points:** 1.

C: That's a lot of people for each zombie to eat. At that rate, they'd be able to devour two and a half cities.

D: 400? If each zombie ate that many, they'd be able to consume ten cities worth of people, not just one!

How to work it out: First, you need to work out how many zombies there will be. This is done by multiplying the average number of graves in each graveyard (5,000) by the number of graveyards in the city (25). This tells you that there are 125,000 graves in total, and that means there will be 125,000 zombies when the dead start to rise. The number of people each zombie needs to devour is then calculated by dividing the population size of the city (5,000,000) by the number of zombies (125,000). When you do this, you get 40. This means each zombie will have to consume, on average, 40 people before the entire city has been devoured.

6. The Injured Friend Problem

What answer did you get?

A: You got it right. You'll arrive at the safe house just half a second before the zombies get to you. Just as well you didn't get it wrong and accidentally go for answer B. **MWZ Points:** 3.

B: Oh no! You got your maths wrong and now your friend's being eaten alive by zombies when you could have made it without abandoning him. You did get the maths wrong, didn't you? You didn't just abandon him, did you? Hmm, I'm not too sure I trust you any more ...

How to work it out: First, work out the time it'll take the zombies to reach the safe house. They can travel at 4 miles an hour, that's 7,040 yards (4 x 1,760, or the number of yards in a mile). This means they will cover the 283 yards to the safe house — the 83 yards between you and the safe house, plus the 200 yards between you and the zombies — in 0.0473 hours. This is worked out by dividing the distance they need to cover (283 yards) by the distance they can travel in an hour (7,040 yards). 0.0473 hours is the equivalent of 2 minutes and 50.3 seconds. You've only got 83 yards to cover, but you're moving much more slowly. You can only cover 1 mile or 1,760 yards in an hour. You will take 0.0472 hours (83/1,760) to reach the safe house. That's 2 minutes and 49.8 seconds, meaning you'll reach safety with just a hair over half a second to spare. If you'd been just one more yard further from the safe house, you'd have had to abandon your friend to have any chance of surviving.

7. The Rapid Fire Problem

What answer did you get?

A: Uh-oh, something went wrong with your calculations. You should have turned and run. Instead, you'll end up as zombie chow.

B: Well done! You got the maths right and because of this, you'll live to fight another day. You must have worked out that you'll only kill 393 of the 400 zombies by the time they get to you. **MWZ Points:** 2.

How to work it out: The machine gun can fire 131 bullets a minute. If you multiply this by the length of time you have to kill all the zombies (10 minutes), you'll find that you can fire 1,310 bullets in that length of time. That would be more than enough bullets if it wasn't for the lack of accuracy. The gun is only 30% accurate. When expressed as a probability, this is 0.3. This means that for every 10 shots fired, you'll only kill 3 zombies. If you multiply the number of bullets you can fire in 10 minutes (1,310) by the probability of each bullet killing a zombie (0.3), you'll find that despite firing over 1,000 bullets, you'll only kill 393 zombies. This means there will be 7 left to overrun your defences.

8. The Quick Draw Problem

What answer did you get?

A: You'd have had enough time so you could have shot the zombie. You might have got the maths wrong, but at least you're still alive.

B: You made the right decision and now there's one less flesh-muncher in the world ... only another 6 billion to go! **MWZ Points:** 2.

How to work it out: The zombie is travelling at 9 miles an hour, but you need to know how long it will take to cover 20 feet. The first thing you need to do is convert the speed from miles an hour to feet per hour. This is 9 times the number of feet in a mile (5,280), which is 47,520. It's only got to travel 20 feet to get to you. If you divide the distance it has to cover (20 feet) number by the number of feet it can travel in an hour (47,520), this will tell you how long it will take to cover this distance. In this case, it's 0.0004209. This figure seems odd, but this is because this is the length of time in hours it will take to travel 20 feet. To convert this number into seconds, you need to multiply it by 3,600 (the number of seconds in an hour). This tells you that at 9 miles an hour the zombie will take 1.51524 seconds to reach you. Since you can draw your gun, aim and fire in 1.5 seconds flat, you'll be able to get your shot off a fraction of a second before it gets to you. You'd better not miss though, because you'll only have one chance to kill it before it reaches you!

9. The Food Supply Problem

What answer did you get?

A: Spot on, but I'm betting that after almost two weeks, you'll never want to taste another piece of Spam as long as you live! **MWZ Points:** 2.

B: You're a bit over there and you'll run out of food a couple of days before you think you will.

C: It might be Spam, but it's not going to last that long.

D: You're out by almost a quarter. If a zombie apocalypse ever comes maybe you'd better leave someone else in charge of the food supplies!

How to work it out: Firstly, don't get confused by the information about the weight of each can. You don't need to know this to work out the answer. Instead, you only need to know the number of calories each can holds (621). You have a total of 56 cans, and each can contains 621 calories. If you multiply these two numbers together (so that's 56 x 621), you get the total number of calories contained in all the cans (in this case, that's 34,776). You then divide this number by the number of calories you need each day (so that's 34,776 divided by 2,500), and this gives you the number of days the food will last for: 13.9. So, sometime on the evening of the 13th day, you're going to finally run out of food. After that, you'll have no choice but to go outside to look for more.

10. The Disappearing Zombies Problem

What answer did you get?

A: Something went wrong with your maths. After only 364 days, there will still be more than 1 million zombies left and you'll almost certainly get eaten!

B: That's a bit too soon. You might get away with it, but there will still be a few zombies wandering around out there.

C: Spot on! The last of the zombies will have rotted away just as you step through the door into the outside world. **MWZ Points:** 2.

D: You've got that wrong. You'll still be huddled in your bunker while all the other survivors are out there staking their claims and rebuilding civilisation.

How to work it out: The starting point here is 7 billion (the number of zombies in the world when you enter the bunker). To work out how many zombies there'll be 28 days later[3], you divide this

---

[3] And now you know why I chose a half-life of 28 days for the zombies!

number by 2. This is 3.5 billion (which is still a lot). After another 28 days, this number will be halved again (giving 1.75 billion). You then repeat this until you get a number that's less than 1. You will need to do this a total of 33 times. This means that it'll take 924 days (28 x 33) before the last zombie will have disappeared. That's 2 years, 6 months, and 13 days (I hope you brought a good book with you!).

11. The Fork In The Road Problem

What answer did you get?

A: Unlucky! The zombies will arrive at the north-west safe house at the same time you do, and this means they'll eat you before you get inside.

B: Unlucky! The zombies will arrive at the north-east safe house at the same time you do, and this means they'll eat you before you get inside.

C: I don't know what went wrong with your maths, but you can't make it to either safe house before the zombies get to you.

D: You're right that it doesn't matter which safe house you head for, but your maths seems to have gone wrong, because you'll reach the safe house at the same time as the zombies.

E: Spot on! You got the right answer, but that's not going to be much consolation to you. As you'll all arrive at the safe house at the same time, you won't have time to get inside so you'll end up dead, despite the fact you did the maths properly. **MWZ Points:** 2.

How to work it out: You need to work out four things to solve this problem: how long it will take you to reach each safe house; and then how long it will take the zombies to reach each safe house. In all cases, the maths is the same. First, you work out the distance that needs to be covered and then divide this by the speed. For example, for you to get to the safe house to the north-east, you need to cover 100 yards, but your speed is only 7.5 miles an hour. First, convert the speed from miles an hour to yards per second. This is done by multiplying the speed by the number of yards in a mile (1,760) and then dividing it by the number of seconds in an hour (3,600). By doing this, you can work out that 7.5 miles an hour is the same as 3.67 yards a second. You then divide the distance you need to cover (100 yards in this case) by this number, and you find you'll reach the north-east safe house in 27.27 seconds. When you do this for the other safe house, you'll find it'll take you 54.55 seconds to reach it. The zombies have to travel further (200 yards to the north-east safe house, and 400 yards to the north-west safe house), but they can also move faster. Travelling at 15 miles per hour, it will take them 27.27 seconds to reach the nearest safe house and 54.55 to reach the one that's further away. This means that no matter which way you go, you and the zombies will all reach the door of your chosen safe house at the same time. This means you're pretty much screwed either way!

12. The Prius vs SUV Problem

What answer did you get?

A: You made the right choice. Despite the fact that it's less fuel-efficient, given the amount of fuel in its tank, you'll be able to get further before you run out. **MWZ Points:** 2.

B: While it might be a good choice for the environment, the Prius is a poor choice in this case. While the Prius is more efficient, meaning it can go further per gallon of fuel, the total distance you can drive using the fuel left in its tank is less than the SUV.

How to work it out: First, how far will you be able to drive in the SUV? To work this out, you begin by calculating how much fuel it has in its fuel tank. The tank can hold 42 gallons when it's full. If it's currently two-thirds full, it will contain two-thirds of 42 gallons. To work out how much this is, divide 42 by 3 and then multiply the answer by 2. This tells you there are 28 gallons of fuel in the SUV's tank. It does 14 miles per gallon, so if you multiply the amount of fuel in its tank (28 gallons) by this number, you will know how far it can travel. In this case, it's 392 miles. Next, you move onto the Prius. Here, you already know the amount of fuel in the tank (9 gallons), so all you need to do is multiply this number by the number of miles it can do per gallon (36). This gives you 324. So despite its better fuel efficiency, the Prius will only get you 324 miles away from the zombie outbreak, while the SUV will get you 392 miles. That's another 68 miles the zombies need to travel to get you, and in a zombie apocalypse that could be the difference between living and dying!

13. The Amputation Problem

What answer did you get?

A: That's right, you only have five seconds to do the maths and amputate your arm before it's too late. **MWZ Points:** 2.

B: You really think you have that long? You'll have turned in almost half that time.

C: Something's gone really wrong with your maths. Luckily (or unluckily), you won't live long enough to work out what.

D: Boy, just how slowly do you think this disease spreads? At this rate, you'll still be reaching for the meat cleaver by the time you turn.

How to work it out: This is a relatively simple calculation. It's just the length of your arm (16 inches) divided by the speed at which the virus spreads along your lymph vessels (2.8 inches per second). This means it will reach the end of your arm in 5.71 seconds. As you can see, the maths here is easy. However, you need to make sure you do it fast and accurately. This is because you'll need to arrive at the right answer quickly enough to take the required action, and you won't have time to double-check your calculation. In real life, this is sometimes the case with maths, and it's the speed at which you can arrive at the right answer that's important, not whether you can do the calculation or not.

This problem is based on how a real disease, rabies, infects the human body. Rabies is probably as close as we get to a real zombie disease because it's spread through bites and turns people into violent, crazed attackers. The virus travels along nerves at a consistent speed, meaning you can work out exactly how long it will take to reach someone's brain once they have been bitten. This is the length of time you have to get medical treatment, because once rabies reaches the brain it is pretty much 100% fatal.

14. The Zombie Abundance Problem

What answer did you get?

A: With that many soldiers, there'd only be 1 for every 138 zombies and they'll be massacred in seconds!

B: That's closer to the right number, but it's still not enough since you'd only have 1 soldier for every 24 zombies. They'll last longer but your troops will still lose in the end.

C: Spot on. You'll have exactly 1 soldier for every 10 zombies, which is just what you need to clear the city without leaving your base unprotected. **MWZ Points:** 2.

D: Since you'll have 1 soldier for every 6 zombies, you'll be sure to win, but because you're sending in more than you need to, you'll risk losing your base if zombies attack ... and that would be a disaster.

How to work it out: The first thing you need to do is estimate the total number of zombies in the city. To do this, you need to account for the zombies hidden in the buildings by multiplying the counts for each city block by five, which you get by adding 1 for the zombie you saw and 4 for the ones that remain hidden from sight. This gives 2,615, 3,160, 3,905, 2,105 and 1,535 as the estimated abundance in each block. Next, you need to work out the average number of zombies in a city block. This is done by adding up the counts in each block and dividing the total by the number of blocks sampled (in this case, 5). This gives an average of 2,664 zombies per city block. You know that there are 142 similar-sized blocks in the city, so if you multiply the average number of zombies per block by this value (142) you will get the estimated abundance for the whole city. In this case, this is 378,288. Now you have the number of zombies, you can work out how many soldiers you need by dividing it by 10 (the required ratio of zombies to soldiers). This gives 37,828.8, or 37,829 if you round it up to the nearest whole number, since you can't send in a fraction of a soldier!

The maths used to solve this problem is the basis of something called Distance Sampling, and it's one of the main ways that conservationists work how many animals are left in a population of an endangered species. This means that this type of maths is not only important when fighting zombies, but also when conserving the planet's biodiversity.

15. The Outrunning Your Friends Problem

What answer did you get?

A: With only 12 friends down, there will still be 1 more zombie chasing you, so you'll still have to outrun 1 more friend to escape.

B: Perfect. You might've lost 13 friends, but at least you got away from the zombies. **MWZ Points:** 2.

C: That's 1 more friend than you need to outrun. You did get the maths wrong, didn't you?

D: Hmm, you do like your friends, don't you?

How to work it out: This is a nice simple one. Each time the pursuing zombies catch someone, the number chasing you goes down by 3. This means all you need to do is divide the number of zombies by 3. In this case, with 37 zombies chasing you, when you divide this by 3, you get 12.33. This means that after 12 of your friends have been caught, there will still be 1 zombie chasing you (it's the 0.33). Therefore, 1 more of your friends has to get caught before you are finally free to escape. So the total number of friends you have to outrun is 13.

16. The Wall Problem[4]

What answer did you get?

A: With 7,884 people, you'll only get 18.25 miles of wall built in time, and that will hardly keep the zombies out, will it?

B: With 15,793 people, you'll only get half the wall built before the zombies get there, and half a wall is little better than no wall at all.

C: That's right. With 31,536 people you'll just get the last brick in place as the zombies reach the wall. **MWZ Points:** 2.

D: With 54,750, you'll get the wall built with plenty of time to spare, but maybe all those extra people could have been doing something else instead?

How to work it out: The first thing you need to work out is how long it will take the zombies to reach you. If you divide the distance they have to travel (125 miles) by the speed they are moving at (3 miles an hour), you'll find it will take the zombie horde 41.67 hours to reach you. This means you have to have the wall finished in 41.67 hours, or — if we divide this by the number of hours in a day; 24 — 1.74 days. Next, you need to work out how many people you would

---

[4] This problem is based on the zombie scenario in the novel *The Outbreak* by Colin M. Drysdale, and also features in the short story *The Wall* by the same author, which can be found in the anthology *Zombies can't swim, and other Tales of the Undead*.

need to finish the wall in this time. 750 people can build 1 mile of wall in a day, but the wall needs to be 73 miles long. If you multiply these two numbers together, you'll find that 54,650 people could build the whole wall in 1 day. Except you have 1.74 days and not just 1 day, so you need to divide this number by 1.74 to get the number you need to complete the wall before the zombies get there, and this is 31,536 people. That's a lot of people, so you'd better start recruiting them right away!

17. The Tank vs Motorcycle Problem

What answer did you get?

A: Bad choice! There's a 35.7% chance of you being caught by a zombie before you reach the safe zone if you choose to travel by tank. This means travelling by tank is marginally more dangerous than travelling by motorbike.

B: Well done, you made the right choice. With a 34.7% chance of being grabbed by a zombie before you get to the safe zone, the motorbike is safer than the tank. **MWZ Points:** 2.

How to work it out: The key to this problem is working out how long it will take to reach the safe zone using each mode of transport. This is done by dividing the distance you need to travel (125 miles) by the speed of each vehicle. For the tank, this is 125/7, which means you'll be on the road for 17.86 hours. For the motorbike, it's 125/60, meaning you'll get to the safe zone in 2.08 hours. Now, you can work out the cumulative probability that you'll be caught by a zombie for each one. For the tank, it's 1-in-50 per hour or, if you convert this into a percentage by dividing 1 by 50 and multiplying it by 100, 2%. To obtain the cumulative probability, you multiply this value by the length of time the journey will take (17.86 hours), which gives you a total chance of falling victim to a zombie before you get to the safe zone of 35.7%. For the motorbike, there's a 1-in-6 chance of a zombie getting you per hour, or if converted into a percentage, 16.67%. When you multiply this by the time it would take you to get there on the motorbike (2.08 hours) this gives you an overall probability of getting killed by a zombie before you get there of 34.7%. Despite the fact that there's a far greater risk of you being caught by a zombie each hour, the motorbike's much faster speed means you spend less time on the road, so overall it's marginally safer.

18. The Zombie Horde[5] Problem

What answer did you get?

A: Oh no! You opened the hatch a minute too soon, meaning there were still zombies all around you. Now they know you're there, you'll never get out alive.

B: Spot on! You opened the hatch just as the last zombie has shuffled past, meaning you can escape back to your safe house before night finally falls. **MWZ Points:** 2.

C. You stayed in the tank a minute too long. You'll be safe from the zombie horde, but you might not make it back to your safe house before it gets dark.

D. Seven minutes? You're way out! You'll never make it back to your safe house in time. Looks like you'll be stuck in the tank all night.

How to work it out: The first thing you need to work out is how long the horde of zombies is. Each city block is 88 yards in length and the zombies stretch for 5 blocks so the whole zombie horde is 5 x 88 yards long. This works out as 440 yards. This means that the last of the zombies are 440 yards away when you close the hatch on

---

[5] This problem is loosely based on a scene from the opening episode of the TV series *The Walking Dead*, where the main character, Rick, becomes trapped in an abandonned tank.

the tank. Next, you need to work out how long it will take all the zombies to stagger past you. To do this, the first thing you need to do is convert the speed from miles an hour to yards a minute. This is done by multiplying the speed in miles an hour (3) by the number of yards in a mile (1,760), to give a speed of 5,280 yards an hour. This number is then divided by the number of minutes in an hour (60) to work out the speed in yards per minute. When you do this, you find out their speed is 88 yards a minute. You can now divide the number of yards the last of the zombies have to travel (440) by this speed (88 yards a minute), to find out that it will take 5 minutes for the last of the zombies to pass your hiding place.

19. The Containment Zone Problem – Part I

What answer did you get?

A: You made the right decision: with 600 men you have more than enough to station 2 every 3 yards around the containment zone's perimeter. **MWZ Points:** 2.

B: You shouldn't have waited for reinforcements because you had enough men. This gave the disease time to spread to other city blocks, so now you need to set up an even larger containment area. All this because you got your maths wrong!

How to work it out: This is a relatively simple calculation, but the trick is doing it in the five seconds you have to make the decision. First, you need to work out the total length of the perimeter of your planned containment zone. The containment zone has 4 sides, each 3 city blocks long, and each block is 50 yards long. To work out the length of the perimeter, you just need to multiply these three numbers together (50 yards per block by 3 blocks per side by 4 sides). This tells you the total perimeter you need to cover is 600 yards. Next, you need to work out the total number of men you'd need to cover it adequately. To do this, you need 2 men every 3 yards. This is the same as saying you need two-thirds of a man per yard, so you divide 600 by 3 and then multiply it by 2, giving a total of 400 men. You have 600, so you have more than enough to set up the perimeter right away, without waiting for reinforcements.

20. The Containment Zone Problem – Part II

What answer did you get?

A: That's the wrong choice. While you had more than enough men to secure a 9-city-block area, you don't have enough to hold the larger containment area, and because of your decision, the city will be lost to the undead.

B: You got it right. You don't have enough men to secure the larger containment area and you need to call for reinforcements right away! **MWZ Points:** 2.

How to work it out: Again, this is a relatively easy one to work out. First, you need to work out the size of the area you need to secure. Originally, you were securing a square of 9 city blocks. This means it was 3 blocks long by 3 blocks wide. If your men pull back 1 block on all sides, this means the area you'll be trying to secure will be a square of 5 by 5 city blocks. As before, this containment zone has 4 sides, but now each side is 5 city blocks long, and each block is 50 yards wide. To work out the length of the perimeter, you just need to multiply these 3 numbers together (50 yards per block by 5 blocks per side by 4 sides). This tells you the total perimeter you need to cover is 1,000 yards. Now you the need to work out the total number of men you'd need to cover this larger perimeter adequately. Just as with the smaller perimeter, you need 2 men every 3 yards. This is the same as saying you need two-thirds of a man per yard, so you divide 1,000 by 3 and then multiply it by 2, giving a total of 667 men (rounded up to the nearest whole man). You only have 600, so the only way you can save the city is to call for reinforcements right away!

21. The Vaccination Programme Problem

What answer did you get?

A: You're way off! You'd need twice as many health professionals to get 95% of the population vaccinated in that amount of time.

B: Your team could only get it done that fast if they worked 24 hours a day, and there's no way they could do that for very long.

C: Something's gone wrong with your calculations, or are you only planning on giving your staff 4 hours off a night? If they don't get enough rest they'll end up making mistakes and you'll miss your target of having 95% of the population vaccinated.

D: Spot on, but if you're going to get enough people vaccinated before there's another outbreak, you'd better get started as soon as possible. **MWZ Points:** 2.

How to work it out: For the vaccination programme to be successful, you need to vaccinate 95% of the population, so the first thing you need to do is work out how many people that is. This is done by multiplying 250 million (the total population size) by 0.95 (95% expressed as a decimal fraction). This tells you you'll need to vaccinate 237.5 million people.

Next, you need to work out how long it will take to vaccinate this many people. It takes 6 minutes to administer each vaccine, so the total time is 6 times the number of people to be vaccinated (237.5 million), which is a staggering 1,425 million minutes. However, this isn't the actual time it will take, because you have 2,500 health workers, all of whom can be working at the same time. To work out the actual time, you need to divide the 1,425 million minutes by the number of workers you have on your team (2,500), and that gives you an actual time of 570,000 minutes, or, if we divide it by 60 (the number of minutes in an hour), 9,500 hours. Each worker can only work 16 hours a day, so to get the number of days it will take, you will need to divide the number of hours required (9,500) by the length of each person's working day (16 hours). This gives you the required length of your vaccination programme in days, which is 593.75 days, or, to round it up to the nearest whole day, 594 days. As you can see, vaccinating a large enough proportion of a population against a disease to make a vaccination programme effective can take a very long time!

22. The Recruitment Problem

What answer did you get?

A: Your maths must have gone wrong. If you only send in 1,600 soldiers, you'll never manage to get the outbreak under control, and the city will be lost within days.

B: Spot on! Just as well you did the maths, or you would have sent in too few troops. In fact, while an initial force of 1,600 men cannot bring the outbreak under control by following your strategy, sending in just 67 more in your initial force would ensure it worked. **MWZ Points:** 3.

C: Whoa, I don't know what happened with your calculations there, but you're way off! Nuking the city will certainly get the outbreak under control, but it'll also needlessly kill an awful lot of innocent people. Maybe, in future, you should double-check your figures before you make quite such a drastic decision.

How to work it out: The maths here is quite complicated, but it reveals something very interesting, honest! To work out the number of zombies at the start of each day, you need to know how many zombies and soldiers there were at the start of the day before. If you know this, you can use the formula $Nt + 1 = (Nt - (St \times 20)) \times 5$ to calculate the number of zombies at the start of any given day. In this formula, St is the number of soldiers at the start of the day before, while Nt is the number of zombies at the start of the preceding day. $Nt + 1$ is the number of zombies there will be at the start of the day itself. The value of 20 is the number of zombies which each soldier will kill during each day, while 5 is the number of people that each zombie will infect every night. Using this formula, you can work out what effect sending in different numbers of troops will have. Start by calculating the number of zombies at the start of day 2 of the campaign (remembering that the number of soldiers will double each day because of the new recruits), and then repeat this for days 3–10. If the number of zombies at the start of a day ever becomes 0, then the zombie outbreak will have been extinguished. If it doesn't, it hasn't.

If you plug in the initial number of soldiers (1,600) and zombies (50,000) into this formula, you'll see that the number of zombies quickly spirals out of control, reaching a whopping 17,088,000 by the start of day 6 ... or more than the entire population of the city. This might make it seem like this strategy would never work, but this isn't true. For example, if you start with 1,700 soldiers and repeat the calculations, you'll see that the zombie problem is sorted in just 4 days. In fact, the difference between success and failure comes down to just a single soldier. If you send in 1,666 soldiers, the city will be overrun by zombies by the start of day 9 of your campaign. In contrast, if you send in 1,667 soldiers, the last zombie will be killed on day 8. This means the 1,667th soldier is an example of what Malcolm Gadwall calls 'a tipping point', where small changes can have big impacts on the final outcome of certain events. It is also an example of a chaotic system where small changes in the starting values can result in very different outcomes further down the road.

23. The Big Freeze Problem

What answer did you get?

A: You're almost right, but the zombies will still be 100 miles away after 4 years and they will have to survive another winter before they can cover these last few miles. This will thin out their numbers even more, meaning there will be many fewer for you to worry about.

B: Spot on! Now you know when the zombies will arrive and how many there will be, you can start preparing for their arrival. **MWZ Points:** 2.

C: I don't know what went wrong there, but you're a few months out, and there will be many more zombies than you're expecting. This means you'll be caught unaware and unprepared when they finally turn up on your doorstep.

D: I don't know how you worked that out, but your poor maths will give you a false sense of security. You'd better double-check your maths before the first zombie lumbers over the horizon and descends on your unsuspecting encampment.

How to work it out: At the start of this problem, the 2 million zombies are frozen in place 1,300 miles to your south. This means they won't be able to start moving until the temperatures warm again next June. During this time, only 30% (or 0.3, if we express this as a decimal fraction) will survive. To work out how many this is, multiply the initial number (2 million) by the percentage expressed as a decimal fraction (0.3). This calculation tells you that at the start of the next summer there will only be 600,000 zombies left. Over the next 3 months, they'll stagger 100 miles each month, or 300 miles in total. So, in exactly 1 year's time, when the zombies freeze up again, there will be a horde of 600,000 zombies 1,000 miles away (the initial 1,300 minus the 300 they've been able to move in the summer months). If you repeat these calculations for the next year, starting with these new values, you'll find that at the end of the second year, the zombies will be 700 miles away and there will be 180,000 of them. At the end of the third year, there will be just 54,000 left and they'll be 400 miles away. At the end of the fourth year, they'll be only 100 miles away, but their numbers will have been whittled down to 16,200. During the next winter, 70% of these zombies will die, meaning there will only be 4,860 still alive to start walking 9 months later, at the beginning of the following June. Since they can cover 100 miles per month, this means these remaining zombies will reach you at the start of July. So in total, you've got 4 years and 10 months to work out a way for you to be able to kill almost 5,000 zombies before any of them get you. Got any ideas?

24. The Six Bridges Problem

What answer did you get?

A: You're wrong, there's no route which will allow you to visit all 4 places and make it back to the safe house without having to use one of the bridges twice. If you set out to try to do it, you'll end up in big trouble!

B: You're right, there's no route which will allow you to get to all 4 locations without crossing a bridge twice. The only decision left now is which place to leave out. **MWZ Points:** 4.

How to work it out: There are two ways to solve this problem. One is trial and error, where you try every single possible route, but that will take time, and in a zombie apocalypse speed is of the essence if you want to survive. The other is to think about it from a mathematical perspective. Each island has one place you want to visit on it. This means that you'll need to be able to reach each island once and leave it once, otherwise you can't get back to where you started. If you go onto an island and can't leave it by a bridge you haven't already used, you'll be stuck. Since you have to cross every bridge on the map at least once to visit all the places you need to go, this means that if any island is connected to other islands by an odd number of bridges, you'll end up getting stuck on it at some point. So, to work out whether it's ever possible to visit every island without using any bridge twice, all you need to do is work out if any of the islands are connected to other islands by an odd number of bridges. In this case, there are two: the big ones to the south-east and the south-west. This means that if you know your maths, you can know instantly that there's no safe route which will allow you to visit everywhere and still get back to the safe house without crossing a zombie-infested bridge ... and that wouldn't be a very good idea.

If you want to explore this problem further, you can try adding another bridge and see how this changes the outcome. If you do this, you'll see that no matter which pair of islands you connect with a new bridge, you can manage to get round all 4 intended destinations and back to your safe house, without having to cross any bridge twice. Why does this make a difference? It's because you no longer need to use every bridge to complete your trip so the rule about needing an even number of bridges attached to each island no longer applies.

If you dig into this even deeper, you'll see that with any number of bridges of 7 and above, as long as each island has at least 2 bridges connecting it to other islands (i.e. so there are no dead ends), you can complete your intended circuit safely, while with any number of bridges of 5 or fewer, there will be at least 1 island only connected to another by a single bridge, meaning you can't do it. Six is the only number of bridges which allows you to have no dead ends, but you are still unable to complete your supply run successfully, and this only works with some placements of bridges and not others. For example, if the upper small island was connected to the big island to its north as its second bridge, rather than the one to the south-west, you'd be able to complete the journey successfully. Again, this is because you no longer have to use all the bridges.

For those who are interested, this problem is based on a rather old puzzle called the 'Königsberg Bridge problem'. This was the first mathematical problem ever solved using Graph Theory, and its original solution by Euler laid the foundations for the field of topology. This makes the Königsberg Bridge problem an important landmark in the history of mathematics.

25. The Colourful Hats Problem

What answer did you get?

A: Whoa, that's not nearly enough different colours! There will be confusion all over the place and your poor choice has put the whole mission in danger.

B: Three colours will work for most of the zones, but there will still be the potential for confusion in the area around zone 17, because 2 neighbouring zones will have to contain soldiers with hats of the same colour. This probably won't endanger the whole mission, but it might slow things down.

C. Spot on. With 4 different colours of hats you can assign every unit a hat colour that will be different from the one worn in every neighbouring zone. **MWZ Points:** 5.

D: That's too many, and you'll have wasted precious time getting hats in a colour that you don't need. Let's hope the zombies haven't multiplied in this time to levels that your men can't handle.

How to work it out: The key to solving this problem is to use something called 'Minimal Criminals'. For this problem, a minimal criminal is the smallest example of a group of zones which shows that you cannot use a given number of colours to successfully assign different hat colours to all neighbouring zones. If you find even one of these minimal criminals on your map for a given number of colours then you cannot successfully assign the coloured hats to each zone.

An example of a minimal criminal which shows that you cannot use just 2 colours of hats (such as red and yellow) is provided at the top of the next page. If you assign red to zone 2, and yellow to zone 1, then you'd have to use a third colour for zone 4, since it touches both of these zones. There are lots of these minimal criminals on this map.

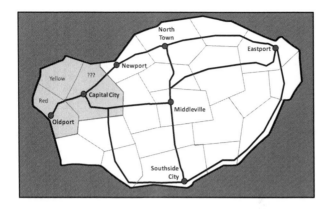

A minimal criminal that shows you cannot use just 3 colours is harder to find, but there is one, and it's shaded in grey on the map below. This consists of a central zone surrounded by 7 other zones. Each of these surrounding zones touches the central zone, so they must have different colours assigned to them. If the zones surrounding it are then assigned alternating colours, you arrive at a situation with the final zone, because it touches the central zone, and zones with each of the 2 other colours cannot use any previously employed colour of hat. This means it has to be given a fourth colour.

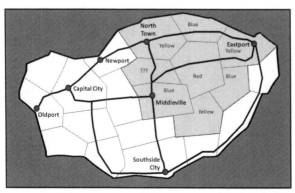

Since there are no minimal criminals, which means you can't use 4 colours, you know that 4 different coloured hats will be enough. In fact, it's impossible to divide the island up into zones which would require more than 4 colours, and this is true of any map. This is known as the 'Four Colour Theorem', and while it was proposed many years ago, it was not proven until 1976 and was the first mathematical theorem which was solved using a computer.

If you want to find out more about the Four Colour Theorem (including the rules for creating the maps and deciding which zones are considered neighbours), visit *en.wikipedia.org/ wiki/Four_color_theorem*.

Part Three

Your
MWZ Score

What Does Your MWZ Score Mean?

As the problems in this book have hopefully shown, your ability to survive a zombie apocalypse will depend on your ability to do maths accurately and quickly. So, based on your total MWZ score, how well are you likely to do?

0: Oh dear. It looks like you'll barely survive long enough to scream 'Zombies!' at the top of your voice before they're munching on your vital organs. At least you now know this will be a problem and you can start doing something about it. After all, you never know when the dead will start to rise.

1–10: The good news is that you won't die immediately if a zombie apocalypse happens tomorrow. The bad news is that, with your level of mathematical skills, the chances are you won't last longer than the first 24 hours. However, take pride in the fact that you are the zombie apocalypse equivalent of cannon fodder (or the men in red uniforms in *Star Trek: The Original Series*), and your inevitable death will help other, more worthy people survive.

11–20: Not bad, but not good either. You'll survive, but probably not beyond the first week, unless you can find someone else who got a better MWZ score to help you stay alive. Maybe you should start hanging out with some *mathletes* instead of your usual crowd. After all, once the dead rise, they'll be the ones who actually have all the answers, and they'll be the ones who manage to keep themselves alive.

21–30: You have about a 50:50 chance of surviving the first month of a zombie apocalypse, but after that, things are going to go down hill fast. Why? Because although you'll be able to deal with the basic problems you're likely to encounter in the immediate aftermath of a zombie apocalypse, you're unlikely to be able to deal with the more complex problems you'll need to solve to survive in the long term.

31–40: Not bad; not bad at all. My assessment is that you might just make it. It's unlikely, but at least it's possible. You've got some good basic maths skills and you can handle a few of the more complex problems, but you can't handle everything. This means you'll eventually get caught out by one of the more complicated situations you'll undoubtedly find yourself in. This sounds harsh, but you've got to face up to the truth. When the dead eventually rise, any gaps in your mathematical knowledge will most likely get you killed, so you'd better start studying some more right now.

41–49: Dude, you're good, but you're not quite perfect. I have no doubt you'll survive, but you're not good enough to make it onto my own personal zombie apocalypse survival team. For that you need a perfect score.

50: Congratulations, you can join my zombie apocalypse survival team, and very few people get this invitation! Give me a call, and I'll tell you where my rendezvous point[6] and my safe house are. That way, you'll know where to find me when the world, as we know it, finally comes to an end!

---

[6] If you don't know what a rendezvous point is, and why it is important to have one in case of a zombie apocalypse, read this blog post: *cmdrysdale.wordpress.com/2013/10/07/the-importance-of-rendezvous-points-in-zombie-apocalypse/*.

About the Author:

Colin M. Drysdale is a scientist with an obsession for recreational mathematics. He is also a big fan of both zombies and the post-apocalyptic survival genre. While he regularly uses maths in his day job as a marine biologist, this book is more a reflection of his interest in maths for maths sake.

As well as writing zombie-based maths problems, he has also written a series of science-based post-apocalyptic survival/zombie novels. These started with his debut novel, *For Those in Peril on the Sea*, and has continued with *The Outbreak* and *The Island at the End of the World,* which are all set in the same post-apocalyptic world. These books are based on many of the places he has visited as part of his job as a marine biologist, and their real-world settings mark them out from many other similar stories.

He now lives in his native Glasgow, where he runs a small business providing mapping advice to ecologists and marine biologists, as well as continuing to write zombie and post-apocalyptic fiction. He is currently working on his fourth book in the *For Those In Peril* series of post-apocalyptic survival of novels.

If you would like find out more about the work of Colin M. Drysdale, visit:

www.ForThoseInPeril.net

Proof

Made in the USA
Charleston, SC
06 November 2015